THE FBI STORY

The FBI and National Security

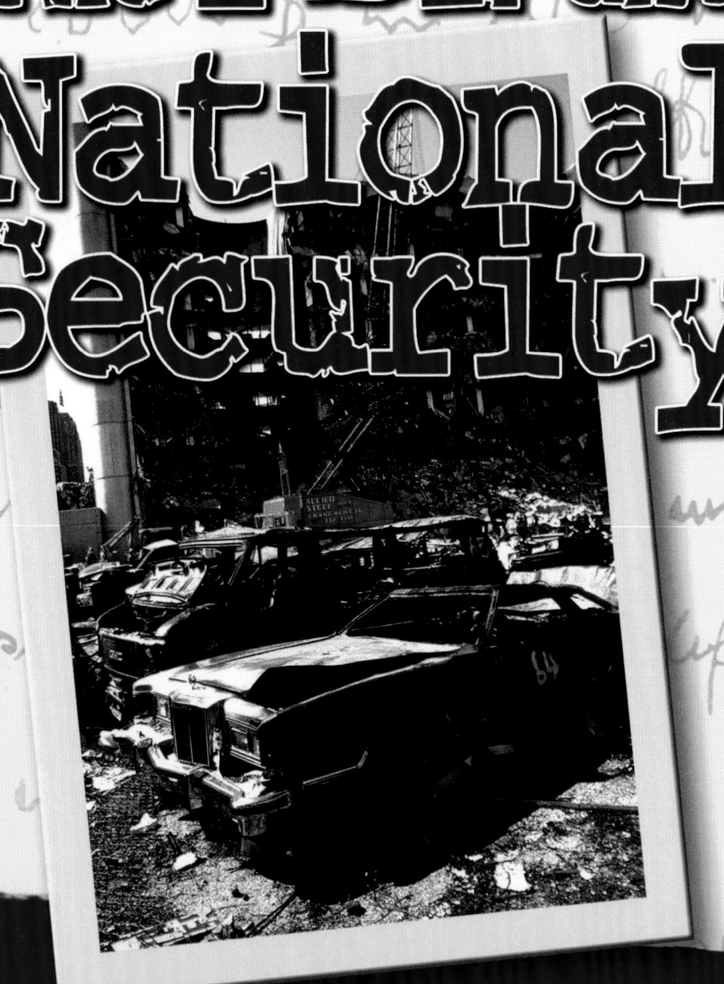

By Robert Grayson

MASON CREST PUBLISHERS

Produced in association with Water Buffalo Books.
Design by Westgraphix LLC.

MASON CREST PUBLISHERS INC.
370 Reed Road
Broomall, Pennsylvania 19008
(866) MCP-BOOK (toll free)
www.masoncrest.com

Printed in the United States of America

First Printing

9 8 7 6 5 4 3 2 1

Library of Congress Cataloging-in-Publication Data

Grayson, Robert.
The FBI and national security / Robert Grayson.
p. cm. — (FBI story)
Includes index.
ISBN 978-1-4222-0564-8 (hardcover) — ISBN 978-1-4222-1371-1 (pbk.)
1. United States. Federal Bureau of Investigation—Juvenile literature.
2. National security—Juvenile literature. I. Title.
HV8144.F43G72 2009
355".033073—dc22 2008050712

Photo credits: © AP/Wide World Photos: 36, 41, 42; © Courtesy of FBI: cover (center, upper right), 7 (right), 9 (all), 13 (both), 19, 28 (right), 30 (both), 38 (both), 48 (upper), 49, 51, 54, 55, 62; © Getty Images: 44 (all); © 2009 Jupiterimages Corporation: 15; Courtesy of the Prints and Photographs Division, Library of Congress: cover (lower right), 7 (left), 14, 16, 25, 26, 27, 28 (left), 35, 46, 60; National Archives and Records Administration: cover (upper left), 22, 32; Used under license from Shutterstock Inc. 4 (both), 53; U. S. Deptartment of Defense: 1, 48 (lower); U.S. Navy: cover (lower left), 7 (right).

Publisher's note:
All quotations in this book come from original sources and contain the spelling and grammatical inconsistencies of the original text.

CONTENTS

CHAPTER 1 The Unthinkable

It was a cool, crisp, sunny, Tuesday morning in September in New York City and Washington, D.C.—hardly an exceptional day, except that on this particular day, the way the United States viewed its place in the world—and national security—would change forever.

There were always those "what if" scenarios. What if the United States was attacked by another country? Worse yet, what if the United States was ever attacked from within its borders? What would be a likely target? How many people might die? Who would be bold enough to do such a thing? Who would think they could carry out such an attack without risking their own lives?

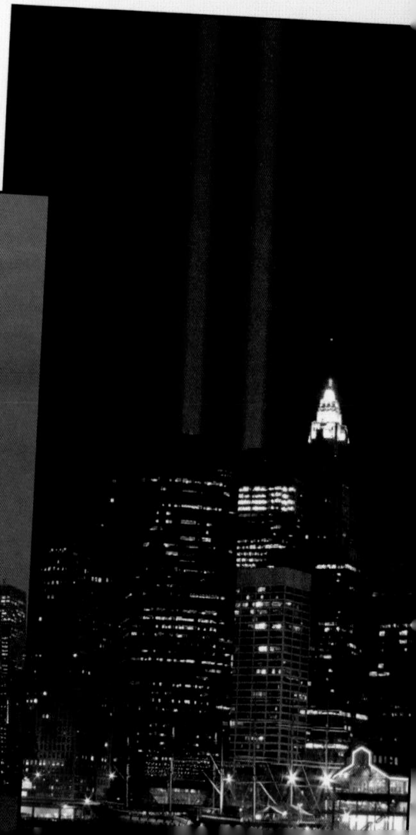

The Twin Towers of the World Trade Center are shown in the photo at left at night before the attacks of September 11, 2001. In the photo at right, two beams of light shine upward from the site after the attacks, marking the spot where the fallen towers once stood and where thousands died.

And who would be bold—and crazy—enough to think they could get away with such an attack without trembling at the thought of retaliation by the most powerful nation on Earth?

9/11: The Day That Changed Everything

The scenarios were frightening, but few Americans could bring themselves to imagine anything resembling what happened on September 11, 2001. On that day, the United States found out it was far more vulnerable than anyone could have imagined. Americans who had once taken for granted their safety and security within their borders were now scared. People wondered how safe they were in their nation's airports, riding public transportation, and working in office buildings.

On that bright September morning, 19 Islamic terrorists boarded four U.S. airliners—unchallenged—and hijacked them. There were several terrorists on each plane, some armed with box cutters. Each group included one hijacker who knew how to take the controls and fly a jumbo jet.

Commercial airliners had been hijacked in the United States before, but the hijackers always had demands—for money or safe passage to some foreign country to seek **asylum**. This was different. This was a suicide mission, designed to kill thousands and leave a permanent scar on the nation's **psyche**, economic system, and way of life. These hijackers were not interested in making a deal; their focus was on death and destruction for its own sake.

Aircraft as Weapons

Using these hijacked aircraft as weapons, the terrorists flew two of the planes into the World Trade Center in New York City. Another was flown into the Pentagon near Washington,

D.C., just as the business day was starting. All those aboard these planes were killed, and many more were killed in the buildings the planes struck. The fourth plane crashed in a field near Shanksville, in rural Pennsylvania, as the crew and passengers battled the terrorists in a desperate attempt to regain control of the plane. That plane was headed for an unknown target, thought to be either the White House or the Capitol in Washington, D.C. All aboard that plane also died.

In New York City, as smoke **billowed** out of the Twin Towers, rescuers worked frantically to save people trapped inside. The scene was similar at the five-story Pentagon. But each tower at the World Trade Center had 110 floors, and people were trapped on the top floors. The first plane hit the North Tower—between the 94th and 98th floors—at 8:46 A.M., just as thousands of people were coming in to work. The second plane smashed into the South Tower at 9:02 A.M., between the 78th and 84th floors. Those in floors above where the planes hit could not escape. It has been estimated that 17,400 people were in the two towers at the time the attacks took place. Most, but not nearly all, got out alive.

Deaths in the Thousands

New York City firefighters, police officers, and other first responders quickly tried to evacuate everyone from the Twin Towers and the buildings around them. Thanks to their heroic efforts, many were saved. By 10:30 A.M., however, before hundreds of thousands of horrified onlookers in New York City and millions more watching on TVs across the world, both towers had collapsed, with several thousand people still trapped inside them at the time. The death toll reached 2,774 people in the Twin Towers that day, including 146 on the two planes that hit them. At the Pentagon, which was struck at 9:37 A.M., 125 people were killed, plus an additional 59 passengers on the plane. Another 40 passengers died in the plane that crashed in Shanksville, Pennsylvania, at 10:03 A.M. A total of 2,998 died during the attacks, with 6,291 injured and countless others left shaken and wondering how such attacks could have happened.

All the terrorists were killed in the coordinated attacks, but they still needed to be identified, which the Federal Bureau of Investigation (FBI) did in a few days. In addition, the FBI wanted to get as much information as it could about the plot, how it was carried out, who was behind it, and if any others were being planned.

Rescuers and investigators walk among the rubble of the World Trade Center during searches for survivors, bodies, and evidence following the attacks of September 11, 2001.

The "9/11" terrorist attacks would turn into the largest investigation in the FBI's history, with 25 percent of the Bureau's special agents and personnel involved in some aspect of the case. Special agents worked around the clock, following leads and tracking down evidence all over the world that eventually linked the radical Islamist group al-Qaeda to the attacks. The FBI also worked to secure the nation during this time of crisis and prevent any additional attacks.

Counterterrorism: The New Priority

The 9/11 attacks transformed the FBI, pushing it forward into a new era in which its priorities were radically changed. Now the prevention of terrorist attacks and safeguarding national security became the Bureau's dominant mission.

The nation would now have to think differently of its relationship with the world around it. As *New York Times* columnist and Pulitzer Prize–winning author Thomas L. Friedman said of the 9/11 attacks:

> The failure to prevent September 11 was not a failure of **intelligence** or coordination. It was a failure of imagination. Even if all the raw intelligence signals had been shared among the F.B.I., the C.I.A. [Central Intelligence Agency], and the White House, I'm convinced that there was no one there who would have put them all together, who would have imagined evil on the scale Osama bin Laden did.

From that day forward, the FBI would have to think in those once-unimaginable terms. The person who was going to lead the FBI through these trying times—and the agency's eventual transformation into an agile, technically savvy organization in the post-9/11 world—was newly appointed Bureau director Robert S. Mueller III.

Mueller had taken over the FBI on September 4, just a few days before the 9/11 attacks. He was going to have to change how the FBI looked at things. He would have to mold the organization into a law enforcement agency that not only makes arrests but also gathers intelligence—on both the national and international levels. All would be focused on preventing any future attacks on the United States.

Intelligence Gathering the Key

The key to stopping terrorism was going to be intelligence gathering and then putting that intelligence to use. The FBI had done this during World War I, World War II, and the Cold War era, a time of mounting tensions between the United States and the **Soviet Union**. During those times, the FBI had spied on people and organizations it felt were enemies within the United States. During the Cold War, for example, the FBI

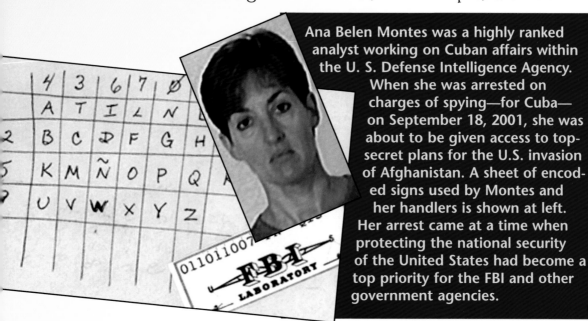

Ana Belen Montes was a highly ranked analyst working on Cuban affairs within the U. S. Defense Intelligence Agency. When she was arrested on charges of spying—for Cuba—on September 18, 2001, she was about to be given access to top-secret plans for the U.S. invasion of Afghanistan. A sheet of encoded signs used by Montes and her handlers is shown at left. Her arrest came at a time when protecting the national security of the United States had become a top priority for the FBI and other government agencies.

focused much of its energy spying on people it felt were **communists**. In more recent years, the Bureau had been focused less on domestic spying and more on making arrests and building strong cases against those it arrested.

Now the FBI would have to begin building strong cases against terrorist suspects it apprehended, to dig up every scrap of available intelligence it could, and to piece them together to uncover the most secretive terror plots against the United States. From that intelligence, the FBI would then launch preemptive strikes and **foil** terror plots before they ever got underway.

After the devastation on 9/11, the FBI became intelligence driven, with every lead relating to terrorism completely followed up and thoroughly investigated. Every one of the Bureau's 56 field offices would consider preventing terrorist attacks its top priority. Each had to be ready to get involved in a terrorism-related case at a moment's notice.

A Shift in Priorities

The shift in priorities meant that Mueller would have to make some tough choices when it came to running the FBI. Local law enforcement agencies had always relied on the FBI to handle certain cases. Now those local agencies would have to step up. They would have to take over investigating local bank robberies, lower-level drug cases, and some fraud cases that the federal agents, or "Feds," had always handled.

The FBI's new concentration on national security and counterterrorism also meant changes within the Bureau itself. First of all, agents would have to be retrained. Then, new agents would have to be hired for their specific skills—

including computer expertise, translation skills, and intelligence analysis know-how. Technology in the Bureau would have to be constantly updated. The FBI would have to have the most up-to-date equipment and technology available in order to stay ahead of terrorists, and special agents would have to be highly skilled at using this equipment and technology. There would have to be better communication and cooperation between agencies such the FBI and the Central Intelligence Agency (CIA). As the FBI began to transform after 9/11, Director Mueller never lost sight of the enemy:

FAST FACTS

The FBI doesn't just collect intelligence from government or law enforcement agencies. The Bureau also relies on private businesses, such as financial institutions, to report any suspicious activity.

> The enemies we face are resourceful, merciless, and fanatically committed to inflicting massive damage on our homeland, which they regard as the **bastion** of evil. In this war, there can be no compromise or negotiated settlement. Accordingly, the prevention of another terrorist attack remains the FBI's top priority as we strive to disrupt and destroy terrorism on our soil.

The FBI in Charge

Following the 9/11 attacks, the FBI expanded its entire counterterrorism operation. FBI headquarters in Washington, D.C., was now overseeing terrorism cases nationwide, so there

A JOINT EFFORT

The FBI's Joint Terrorism Task Forces (JTTFs) were in place long before the terror attacks of September 11, 2001. The first one was established in New York City in 1980. It included 10 FBI special agents and 10 members of the New York City Police Department.

The number of JTTFs had grown to 35 before 9/11. They were spread all across the United States. After the attacks, JTTFs were opened in all 56 of the FBI field offices and in many major cities throughout the country. Today there are more than 106 JTTFs, and 3,723 law enforcement officials work on the teams.

The new JTTFs are made up of both FBI special agents and members of other federal agencies. These other agencies include the Department of Homeland Security, U.S. Immigration and Customs Enforcement, the U.S. Secret Service, the U.S. Coast Guard, the CIA, and the Transportation Security Administration (TSA). People from other federal, state, and local law enforcement and intelligence agencies may also be included.

The people assigned to the JTTFs are highly trained. They have a variety of intelligence, law enforcement, and computer skills. Teams are made up of investigators, SWAT experts, language specialists, intelligence analysts, explosives specialists, and financial experts, just to name a few of these dedicated crime fighters.

The efforts of these local JTTFs are coordinated through the National Joint Terrorism Task Force (NJTTF). It is headquartered in the FBI building in Washington, D.C. The NJTTF draws its members from every federal agency that collects intelligence.

The local JTTFs have established good ways to exchange information and findings about suspected threats. They share that information among JTTF members as soon as it is gathered. JTTFs have responded to all sorts of cases, including letters containing **anthrax**, fake ID operations, and the transportation of deadly weapons and explosives.

Like the FBI, JTTFs do not close on weekends and holidays. The task forces operate every day of the year. This way, they can respond to any suspected threat right away.

would be no doubt about which agency was in charge of these cases. The FBI would be held accountable.

To accomplish its goal of stopping terrorists before they strike, the FBI first doubled and then tripled its multiagency local Joint Terrorism Task Forces (JTTFs) across the country. The FBI backed those local task forces with a new National Joint Terrorism Task Force (NJTTF). From the Bureau's headquarters in Washington, D.C., it feeds local JTTF teams the latest intelligence about ongoing terror-related investigations.

Following the Money

The FBI also put together a team of financial experts to track terrorists' money trails. Team members watch when large sums of money move around among known terrorists or terrorist organizations. Whenever possible, the FBI tries to **freeze the assets** of people or groups that have terrorist connections.

Even with all these changes, the FBI knows that to fight terrorists the agency must keep getting even better at gathering intelligence; and it must make more associations with other nations that are also fighting terrorism. With enemies who are willing to let themselves be killed as part of their battle plan, the fight promises to be a tough one.

The National Joint Terrorism Task Force is made up of representatives from 35 federal agencies. The vehicles shown here were on standby as part of the FBI's contribution to the multiagency effort to keep the nation's capital safe during the inauguration of President Barack Obama in January 2009.

CHAPTER 2 A Matter of National Security

On September 6, 1901, an angry, out-of-work factory worker focused the nation's attention on national security. Just as the attacks on 9/11 would do—almost 100 years later to the day—his actions left people wondering if the nation was really secure and who was making sure of that.

This newspaper photo, dated September 9, 1901, shows assassin Leon Czolgosz in his jail cell just days after he had shot President William McKinley. The newspaper published the photo with this caption: "THE WRETCHED ANARCHIST WHO SHOT THE PRESIDENT."

Hatred Fueled by Anger

The factory worker was Leon Czolgosz. The 28-year-old Ohio man had been unemployed for several years. During his layoff from work, Czolgosz spent his time reading the writings and attending the speeches of leading anarchists. Anarchists are against most forms of authority, particularly government. In modern human history, many anarchists have preached—and some have used—violence as a means to bring down governments they oppose. Czolgosz took on their point of view.

FAST FACTS

When President William McKinley was killed in 1901, he became the third U.S. president to be assassinated, following Abraham Lincoln (in 1865) and James Garfield (in 1881). In 1963, John F. Kennedy would become the fourth.

This illustration shows the shooting of President William McKinley (at right, wearing a white shirt) by Leon Czolgosz (shown with his hand wrapped in white). McKinley had just walked into the Pan-American Exposition in Buffalo, where security was, by today's standards, relatively light.

In August 1901, Czolgosz read in a newspaper that President William McKinley would be touring the Pan-American Exposition in Buffalo, New York, on September 6. After reading the article, Czolgosz took a train to Buffalo. When he arrived in the city, he bought a handgun and went to kill the president. Czolgosz later told police that he simply felt McKinley had too much power over too many people. The assassin shot McKinley in the stomach at close range at about 4:00 P.M. on September 6. It happened just as the president walked into the exposition to greet people. McKinley died of his wounds eight days later, and Vice President Theodore Roosevelt became the president.

The First Terrorists

As the nation recovered from the shock of McKinley's assassination, it became apparent to law enforcement groups that the threat represented by this crime went far beyond questions of security in one U.S. city. In the early days of the 20th century, anarchists gathered in small groups, called cells, to spread their ideas. Because they sometimes used violence to

Charles J. Bonaparte, grandnephew of the French emperor Napoleon Bonaparte, was the attorney general under President Theodore Roosevelt. He helped create what would become the FBI.

further their cause, anarchists had become, in the view of many local law enforcement officials, the first modern-day terrorists to operate on a national scale.

On top of this, the country had grown and now stretched from coast to coast. At this point, there was no organization whose members had the training to guard the entire nation from both outside attack and crimes from within its own borders. The timing seemed perfect for an agency such as today's FBI to come into existence to gather intelligence and put a stop to plots that threatened national security. President Theodore Roosevelt supported the establishment of a national crime-fighting force. In 1906, the charge to create such a force fell to Attorney General Charles J. Bonaparte.

The First National Crime-Fighting Force

Bonaparte was frustrated when he became the nation's top lawman. Only then did he find out that he would have to fight crime and ward off any threats to the nation all by himself. He had no investigators of his own. If Bonaparte wanted to use an investigator on a federal case, he had to borrow one from the U.S. Secret Service. Those investigators reported to the Secret Service chief, not to the attorney general.

Bonaparte complained to the U.S. Congress about the problem. Doing this only made matters worse for him, however. Congress responded by banning him from using Secret Service agents for his investigations. The lawmakers feared that the attorney general and the president were trying to expand their powers. Bonaparte felt blocked at every turn. So, with the backing of the president, he began hiring his own investigators in 1908.

This marked the birth of the FBI. At the time, however, it was not called the FBI. The agency was known as the Bureau of Investigation (BOI).

At first, Bonaparte's agents, some of whom had been working for the Secret Service, had a small but important role in national security. They also gathered information on the activity of anarchists and arrested people involved in **treasonous** activity. The Bureau also became involved in national security on other fronts, such as crimes that took place along the nation's borders, including illegal immigration and smuggling between the United States and Mexico.

Who Was in Charge?

World War I began in 1914. Just before that, the Secret Service and the Bureau of Investigation got into a **turf war**. In this struggle, the agencies needed direction. It was no longer clear which agency was in charge of intelligence gathering for the nation.

The rivalry caused friction between the two agencies. The Secret Service had been around for almost 50 years and the BOI was less than six years old, but neither agency had much **counterintelligence** experience or special skill in investigating these kinds of cases. When World War I broke out, however, the United States needed all the help it could get to protect the country from threats from within its borders, usually in the form of espionage (spying to steal information) and **sabotage**.

At the start of this war, the United States had not chosen sides and so was officially neutral. Despite President Woodrow Wilson's declaration that "[t]he United States must be neutral in fact, as well as in name, during these days that are to try men's souls," Germany periodically sent **saboteurs** to bomb **munitions** plants on U.S. soil. The BOI was to investigate these security threats, one of which occurred on a Sunday morning, July 30, 1916, in Jersey City, New Jersey.

Sabotage on the Home Front

Early that morning, German agents broke into the Black Tom railroad yard, which was located on the Jersey City waterfront. The yard was used as a storage center for munitions made in the northeastern United States. Germany feared that the United States would sell the munitions to the Allied forces, which were led by Britain and France. In World War I, these countries fought the Central Powers—Germany, Austria-Hungary, and the Ottoman Empire, which was based

This grainy image is one of the few photographs of the aftermath of the Black Tom railroad yard explosion in Jersey City, New Jersey. The explosion, set by German agents before the United States had entered World War I, helped set the stage for U.S. entry into the war. It also thrust the Bureau of Investigation (later to be known as the FBI) into the fight to protect U.S. national security within the borders of the United States.

in Turkey and spanned much of southeastern Europe, the Middle East, and North Africa.

The German agents blew up train cars filled with 1,000 tons of munitions. The explosions turned the sky over New York Harbor bright orange and blew windows out of buildings in both Jersey City and Lower Manhattan, less than 2 miles (3.2 kilometers) away. Lower Manhattan, which would one day become the site of the World Trade Center and a target of the attacks of September 11, 2001, rocked in response to the explosions.

Thousands of people rushed onto the streets as debris rained down. The Brooklyn Bridge, which was not far away from the scene of the bombings, also shook. **Shrapnel** lodged in the Statue of Liberty. A tremor from the blasts was felt in Philadelphia, over 100 miles (160 km) away.

The blasts in the railroad yard sent shock waves to Ellis Island, where immigrants waited to enter the country. The blasts destroyed 87 railroad cars, six piers, and 13 warehouses in the railroad yard and spread panic through the streets of Jersey City. When the blasts ended, all that remained of the Black Tom railroad yard was a gaping hole reaching below sea level. John Gallo, who was chief engineer on the *Sledington,* a tugboat working in New York Harbor at the time of the Black Tom explosions, said the blasts were so powerful that they lifted the tug out of the water. "I never believed such a thing could be. It rained fire all about us," he reported.

Death, Destruction, but No Justice

Seven people were killed by the blast, and hundreds more were injured. Among those killed was a sleeping baby who was at home and thrown out of his crib by the blast. Damage was estimated at $20 million at the time. This is the equivalent of about $375 million in today's dollars. The Bureau investigated the case, but the United States had few laws covering national security, and those laws were weak. That combined with the small size of the BOI staff at the time (just 260 employees) made it difficult for the BOI to gather very much useful evidence.

No one was ever found guilty of setting the bombs. But enough evidence was gathered to firmly link Germany to the crime. Agents even had the names of German suspects who had fled the United States after the blast. The full investigation took years to complete and went on long after the end of World War I. Some consider the bombing the first major terrorist attack on the United States. In 1939, the United States demanded $50 million in **restitution** from Germany. By then, however, World War II had broken out and would soon put the United States at odds with Germany once again. The matter was not officially settled until 1979—more than 60 years after the blast. At that time, the government of West Germany agreed to pay all outstanding war claims.

The attack on the Black Tom railroad yard was one of the worst acts of sabotage by Germany at the time. But it was certainly not the only one. The BOI found that many factories throughout the country were targets of unexplained explosions. All of these were eventually linked to German sabotage. Investigations of these incidents proved one thing conclusively: The United States needed tougher laws to deal with national security.

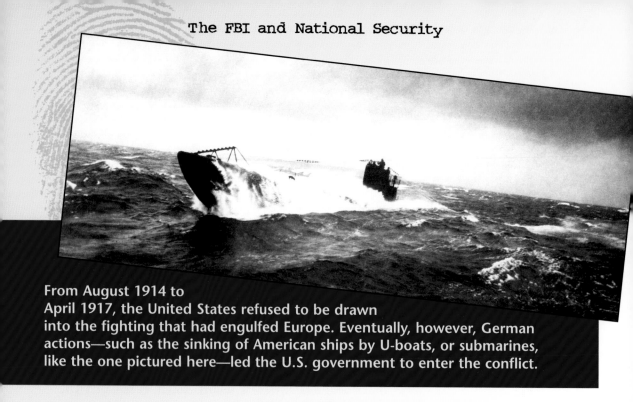

From August 1914 to April 1917, the United States refused to be drawn into the fighting that had engulfed Europe. Eventually, however, German actions—such as the sinking of American ships by U-boats, or submarines, like the one pictured here—led the U.S. government to enter the conflict.

Beefing Up Counterterrorism Laws

Germany continued to sink U.S. ships in international waters during the early years of World War I. This went on even though the United States was still officially neutral.

Eventually, the United States had had enough. The United States declared war on the Central Powers on April 6, 1917, and entered World War I. That June, Congress passed the Espionage Act of 1917, and the BOI had the job of enforcing it. That made the Bureau the lead agency in protecting national security. That job included policing enemy aliens. This meant that agents had to watch Germans who lived in the United States but were not U.S. citizens and were seen as a possible threat to U.S. security.

The BOI also rounded up army deserters and conducted counterintelligence operations. The Bureau scored a major triumph in its intelligence gathering in 1917, when its agents discovered that Germany had hidden important documents in the Swiss Consulate in New York City. These documents contained information about Germany's war activities. This included reports about German spying in the United States during the war. The material also showed how Germany was getting weapons to its allies. The papers stated that Germany was loading munitions on ships belonging to neutral countries. Ships from neutral countries were supposed to be able to sail through international waters without being fired on by either side.

The problem was this: How would the BOI get the documents out of the Swiss Consulate? Five agents were assigned to the case. They learned that the documents were locked in a ninth-floor storage room in the consulate building. The agents, posing as businessmen, rented office space in the consulate adjacent to the storeroom. In the evenings, after consulate employees went home, the agents worked on a tunnel between their office and the storeroom. Once the tunnel was completed, the agents entered the storeroom. There they found the secret documents sealed in trunks and boxes. Over the next few months, the men went through the documents. They took the ones they needed and then resealed the trunks and cases.

Employees at the consulate never suspected a thing. But the documents taught the United States a great deal about enemy activity in the United States. The Bureau's action also proved that it had what it took to be a major force in intelligence gathering. The country now knew the Bureau was up to the task of protecting national security. It would not be long before the agency's skills in counterintelligence work would be tested again.

CHAPTER 3 Lessons Learned; Challenges Faced

World War I ended in November 1918. But the world was still in turmoil. In 1917, Russia came under control of the Bolsheviks, a revolutionary group that would eventually turn Russia into a communist state and draw several other republics into its fold. The U.S. government was worried about the Bolsheviks' threat of worldwide revolution. That fear was fueled by a series of bombings in 1919.

Mail Bombs

In late April 1919, about 30 bombs were mailed to well-known U.S. citizens. These citizens included judges and elected officials. The first few bombs were delivered before the U.S. Post Office was told to watch for the suspicious packages, so some of the mail bombs reached their destinations. One bomb that got through went to the home of U.S. Senator Thomas W. Hardwick of Georgia. The senator's wife and housekeeper were injured when they tried to open the package.

On June 2, 1919, eight bombs were set off—at the same time—in eight cities across the United States. The bombs again targeted prominent people. One of those bombs exploded outside the home of newly appointed U.S. Attorney

People stand in front of the home of Attorney General Alexander Mitchell Palmer following the explosion of a bomb placed outside his house. In the early decades of the 20th century, the threat of property damage, injury, and death due to explosive devices had become a terrifying reality to Americans.

General Alexander Mitchell Palmer in Washington, D.C. Palmer wasn't hurt, but he was shaken by the blast and his home was heavily damaged.

None of the people targeted were hurt or killed by the bombs. But a police officer and a woman passing one of the victim's homes were killed when the bombs went off. Palmer knew that the nation would demand a response to the attacks. So he used the Department of Justice and the BOI to begin an investigation and put an end to the terror.

Call for Eternal Vigilance

After the Black Tom explosions, New York City Police Commissioner Arthur Woods saw that changes needed to be made:

> The lessons to America are clear as day. We must not again be caught napping with no adequate national intelligence organization. The several federal Bureaus should be welded into one, and that one should be eternally . . . **vigilant**.

Thinking and acting along those same lines, Attorney General Palmer created a new division within the Justice Department. This division's job was to gather intelligence on anyone living in the United States who might threaten the nation. Palmer included in this group radicals, anarchists, people with communist ties, and others. Palmer said the job of the special division was to "tear out the radical seeds that have entangled American ideas in their poisonous theories." Palmer was certain that Russian agents were working within the United States.

The division was to gather its own intelligence. It would then combine its information with information other government agencies had already collected. Palmer put a young Justice Depart-ment lawyer by the name of John Edgar Hoover in charge of the new division. Hoover gathered information on

An overturned vehicle lies amid the rubble of a terrorist bombing on Wall St., the heart of New York City's financial district, on September 16, 1920. The bombing was another act of terrorism on U.S. soil that underscored the need to strengthen the nation's intelligence and security systems.

THE WALL STREET BLAST

On September 16, 1920, a horse-drawn wagon was traveling along Wall Street in Lower Manhattan. It was lunchtime, and hurried workers poured onto the street. The wagon stopped across the street from the J.P. Morgan Bank. The driver got out and abandoned the wagon. Within minutes, it exploded. Chaos reigned over the financial district as people lay wounded and dying all over one of New York City's busiest thoroughfares.

Some newspapers speculated that the attack was an act of war, though no one knew who was responsible for it. The death toll kept rising throughout the day. In the end, 38 people had been killed and 400 were injured. The blast caused $2 million in property damage.

Leaders of the New York Stock Exchange did not want anyone to think that a terrorist attack could close down the exchange. So they decided to reopen the next day. City workers rushed to clean up the damaged area and, unfortunately, disposed of a lot of evidence in the process.

The Bureau of Investigation (BOI) was called in on the case. Agents investigated the scene for what little evidence they could find after the cleanup. It was not immediately apparent that the explosion was a terrorist act, but flyers found in the area of the bombing demanded the release of people referred to in the flyers as political prisoners who were then being held in U.S. jails. The Bureau conducted hundreds of interviews in connection with the case and eventually pieced together enough evidence to conclude that the blast was the work of radical anarchists. By then, however, whoever had committed the crime had fled the country, and no arrests were ever made. Fear gripped the Wall Street area for some time after the bombing, as the country's national security was challenged once again.

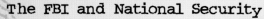

Attorney General Alexander Mitchell Palmer (left). His practice of making mass arrests in the name of national security became known collectively as the Palmer Raids. The public turned on him and his raids (carried out between 1919 and 1921) when it became known that he had been sidestepping federal laws. Hundreds of people had been arrested on made-up charges, some held for months without trial, while others had been deported without hearings. It fell on J. Edgar Hoover (above right), who became head of the Bureau of Investigation in 1924, to balance the need to conduct matters related to national security with the Bureau's role as a federal police agency.

thousands of people. With Palmer's blessing and the help of the BOI, he started making arrests in 1919.

The arrests, called the Palmer Raids, went on between 1919 and 1921. Raids were carried out in 30 cities, and most of the people arrested were aliens. The raids were carried out without warning or warrants. Some people were held in jail for months without a trial. About 250 people were deported without proper hearings. At first, the public sided with Palmer. Then word got out that many people had been arrested on trumped-up charges. People's civil liberties were being violated. Public opinion changed as people began to view the raids as **unconstitutional**.

Guarding Civil Liberties

Now it was the Justice Department that was under a cloud of suspicion. The raids stopped. The Bureau continued its work in national security, however, making sure that it followed the laws of the land as it gathered intelligence and made arrests.

During the rest of the 1920s and into the early 1930s, the

BOI continued to investigate national security breaches. With the rise of crime nationwide during the era of Prohibition (when manufacturing and selling alcoholic beverages was outlawed), the agency was also busy cracking down on major criminals and gangs. As the Bureau pursued and built cases against these criminals, it became a finely tuned investigative unit. It was led by the same man who had run Palmer's intelligence unit at the Justice Department: J. Edgar Hoover.

Hoover took over the BOI in 1924. It was then that the agency started chasing lawbreakers as well as keeping its eye on activities in Russia. In December 1922, Russia joined with several other republics to create the Union of Soviet Socialist Republics (USSR). At the time, the USSR, or Soviet Union, was the largest nation under communist rule. The BOI wanted to make sure communism did not spread to the United States.

Concerns About Germany and Japan

The Bureau had a lot to do watching the developments in the new USSR. But it also began watching activities in Germany, where a ruthless leader, Adolf Hitler, took over in 1933. Hitler brought the Nazi (National Socialist) Party to power. In the 1930s and 1940s, the Bureau began investigating people living in the United States who might be spies and saboteurs for other countries. High on the list of suspected countries were Germany and the Soviet Union, although the USSR would soon become an ally of the United States in its fight against Germany in World War II. In 1934 President Franklin D. Roosevelt asked the Bureau—now called the Division of Investigation (DOI)—to gather intelligence on Nazi groups in the United States. These groups included the German

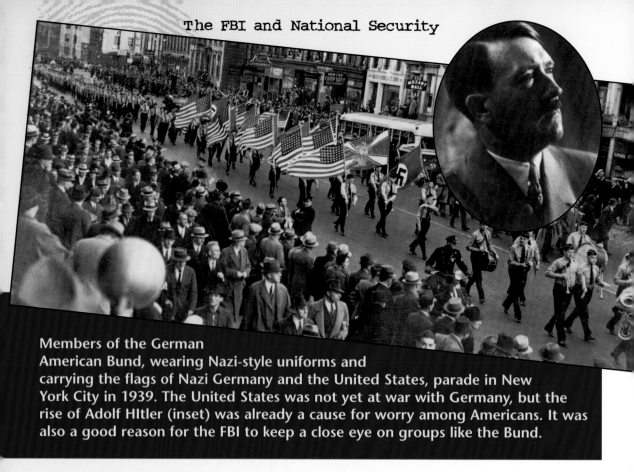

Members of the German American Bund, wearing Nazi-style uniforms and carrying the flags of Nazi Germany and the United States, parade in New York City in 1939. The United States was not yet at war with Germany, but the rise of Adolf HItler (inset) was already a cause for worry among Americans. It was also a good reason for the FBI to keep a close eye on groups like the Bund.

American Bund and the Silver Shirts. Roosevelt wanted to know if these groups were working with foreign agents.

In 1936 Roosevelt ordered Hoover to have the agency gather intelligence on all **fascist** and communist groups. Special agents were also given orders to check out any Japanese organizations that might be helping Imperial Japan spy on the United States. By this time, Japan was preparing to invade China. That invasion began in 1937, and Japan later allied itself with Nazi Germany during World War II. At this point, the DOI had been renamed the Federal Bureau of Investigation (FBI). Several agencies had their own divisions of investigation, and government officials felt that the Bureau needed a name that would make it stand out above the rest.

The FBI operated as a national law enforcement agency during the build-up to World War II. It put together a team of local law enforcement officials to keep special agents informed about unusual activity around the country. The Bureau was also developing contacts around the world, especially in Canada and Britain. The Central Intelligence Agency (CIA), which would become the nation's leading spy agency, did not exist at the time, so the FBI became the lead agency in counterintelligence and gathering intelligence overseas.

Cracking a Major German Spy Ring

From the late 1930s to 1941, when the United States entered World War II, the FBI uncovered more than 50 German and Japanese spy operations in the United States. This included a spy ring run by German master spy Fritz Duquesne. The legendary Duquesne, known by code names like Black Panther and Dunn, had completed many missions for Germany. But he and members of his spy ring were caught passing secret documents to an FBI double agent. Duquesne and 32 members of his ring were arrested in June 1941. All 33 were convicted of espionage. Hoover called it the greatest spy roundup in history, and it remains the largest spy conviction in U.S history to this day. Germany later admitted that the arrests broke the back of its spy operation in the United States.

Japan bombed Pearl Harbor in Hawaii—the home of the U.S. Pacific fleet—on December 7, 1941. Shortly after that, the United States entered World War II. The country declared war on the Axis powers and joined forces with the Allies. The FBI was ready. J. Edgar Hoover had a plan in place to mobilize the Bureau in the event of war, and he now put the plan into action.

Before the United States declared war, the FBI had been tracking aliens living in the United States. The Bureau was interested in people who posed a threat to the nation's security. The night of December 7, with an executive order from President Franklin D. Roosevelt, the Bureau began arresting some of these people and handing them over to the Immigration Department for hearings. The FBI had learned a lesson from the Palmer Raids, however. Agents were careful to make sure that these arrests were handled properly. They made sure no one's civil liberties were violated. More than 3,800 aliens were taken into custody within a 72-hour period after the Pearl Harbor bombing.

Refusing Roosevelt's Order

President Roosevelt had issued another order for the FBI. He wanted a wide-scale roundup of Japanese Americans. The government feared that some of these people might side with Japan in the war. But Hoover did not want to follow this order. He believed that the FBI had already arrested anyone who was a real threat. When Hoover refused to follow the president's **internment** order, Roosevelt ordered the military to carry out the operation instead.

Japanese Americans are shown boarding a bus to one of the camps where hundreds of thousands of Americans of Japanese descent were held during World War II. The forced relocation to internment camps was carried out without the cooperation of J. Edgar Hoover, who felt that these U.S. citizens did not pose a security threat.

Still, the FBI was very active during World War II. Agents continued gathering intelligence to protect the homeland and to prevent Nazi saboteurs from attacking installations on U.S. shores. They spent time tracking companies that deliberately sold defective war materials to the United States at a large profit. The FBI crime laboratory was growing, too. It played a big role in breaking enemy codes and helped devise ways to intercept enemy communications. In every way, the Bureau was now key to protecting national security, and the government had come to depend on the agency doing that job.

A New Enemy

World War II ended in 1945. But the FBI's job in counterintelligence did not. Almost immediately, the FBI had to turn its attention to secret agents. The Bureau

Vol. XX No. 6

Publisher

October, 1938

MECHANIX ILLUSTRATED

Edgar Hoover
s how science
netrates the
k corners of
inality to re-
solutions not
re known in
enforcement.

by
ley Gerstin
nterview with

G-MEN
Fight Crime
With Science
J. Edgar Hoover

AUGUST 16, 1937, two men

The FBI's world-class forensics laboratory, which helps with national security and counterterrorism investigations, started as a small technical lab in 1932 and steadily grew through the years. This magazine interview with Director J. Edgar Hoover, published in 1938, had this to say about the lab: "With microscope, ultraviolet lamp, test tubes, spectrograph, refractometer and parallel light rays, science tracks down America's most vicious criminals. Bloodstains, human hairs, scrapings from under fingernails, burnt letters and threads of cloth tell tales of the dead to scientists trained in crime detection."

believed the Soviet Union had many people carrying out spy missions in the United States. The Soviet Union had been an ally to the United States in World War II in the fight against Nazi Germany. The two nations had radically different political and economic systems, however, and these differences had been an object of friction between them up to the war. Now, with the war over, the traditional distrust between these two emerging superpowers grew even stronger, and the FBI was about to find out that the Soviet Union had a leg up on the United States when it came to spycraft.

This came out when Soviet code clerk Igor Gouzenko defected to Canada in late 1945. Gouzenko gave the FBI some much-needed insight into the USSR'S intelligence-gathering methods. Gouzenko, who worked in the Soviet embassy in Ottawa, Ontario (Canada), was upset with his homeland. He learned that the Soviets were going to ask him to return from Canada to the Soviet Union for good. But Gouzenko had found life in Canada better than that in his homeland. He didn't like the political climate in the Soviet Union at the time, either.

Gouzenko decided to defect to the West, and he brought many valuable documents with him. Among these were codebooks that exposed the espionage activities of the Soviet Union during World War II. He first went to the Royal Canadian Mounted Police, and they, in turn, called in the FBI. After reviewing the documents Gouzenko handed over, the Bureau could see that the Soviets posed a significant threat to national security in the United States. The Cold War was on.

TO CATCH SOME SPIES

FBI special agents made huge contributions during World War II. But the story of their brave actions is almost lost today.

By 1940, Nazi spies were using Latin America as a staging ground. From here, they ran missions into the United States to gather information about the country's readiness for war. Brazil and Argentina were home to more than 500,000 German immigrants. Many of these people were loyal to the Nazis. This made these countries a perfect area for spies to settle. It was easy for them to live there without seeming to be out of place.

To fight this dangerous situation, the FBI created, at the request of President Franklin D. Roosevelt, the Special Intelligence Service (SIS) in 1940. For the next seven years, over 340 FBI special agents and support staff worked undercover in South and Central America.

It was a tough role at first. Special agents had to master mannerisms and foreign languages (such as Spanish and Portuguese) to fit into their new surroundings. They had to gain the trust of their new neighbors. But they did it. The undercover agents intercepted information that Nazi sympathizers were gathering to give to Nazi spies. Sometimes they were even able to arrange for the Nazi spies to get incorrect or useless information, instead of the real intelligence they were seeking.

The undercover FBI agents identified more than 887 German spies and 30 saboteurs. The agents also captured 40 radio transmitters. The German spies used these to get information to other German agents in Europe. Some of the information that the FBI gathered from all of this work helped the nation's European allies.

The SIS eventually became a separate agency from the FBI. From then on it was known as the CIA. But the FBI had made a major contribution to U.S. efforts during World War II. And along the way, the Bureau learned some valuable ways to gather intelligence and protect national security.

These FBI special agents are shown engaging in electronic surveillance in the 1940s. They were typical of the type of undercover agents that spied on Nazi sympathizers in Latin America during World War II.

CHAPTER 4 The Chill of Cold War

The Cold War lasted from 1945 to 1991. This was a period of high tension, conflict, and competition between the United States and the Soviet Union. It was highlighted by weapons development and competition, a nuclear arms race, massive military spending, dire threats, and propaganda. National security was always at stake. Some of the Cold War's key weapons, espionage and intelligence gathering, put the FBI right in the middle of the fray.

Sleeper Agents

In 1945, the FBI learned about an intelligence tool the Soviets were using—sleeper agents or cells. Sleeper agents

When Igor Gouzenko defected from the Soviet Union in 1945, he gave the FBI some important information about the Soviets' use of sleeper agents and sleeper cells. He is shown here wearing a hood to conceal his identity during an interview in Canada in 1954.

are spies who move to a target country. There they work their way into the community. They have no immediate mission. Their only task is to become part of the fabric of a neighborhood, get a job, make friends, and blend into the local scene. Because they have no **imminent** assignment, they are thought of as having gone to sleep. But, in reality, they are waiting for the country to call on them for a spy mission at a later time.

FAST FACTS

Sleeper agents are popular in fiction. The popular counterterrorism action thriller TV show *24* has used sleeper agents in its plot lines.

The FBI moved quickly on their information. With intelligence specialists from Canada and the United Kingdom (Britain), FBI agents rooted out Soviet spies from within the United States, Canada, and the UK. Many of these sleeper agents had been in these countries a long time. Some had even managed to get government jobs in offices that contained secrets they were able to steal.

FBI special agents quickly learned a lot about how sleeper agents work. With this knowledge, agents were able to rid the U.S. government of these secret Soviet agents by the early 1950s. As a result of this operation, the FBI forced the USSR to retool the way it handled its spying missions against the West.

A Bizarre Case in the 1950s

While working in the national security arena, the FBI has handled many interesting cases. Through these, the Bureau has discovered that foreign agents can be very creative in their work. In the spring of 1953, a man bought a newspaper from a newsboy on a street corner in Brooklyn, New York.

As the man walked away with his newspaper, the newsboy dropped the nickel the man had given him. The coin split in half. The boy could see a piece of film lodged in one half of the coin. He gave the coin to the New York City Police Department, and the police gave it to the FBI. FBI agents saw that the film had a series of numbers on it. They recognized that it was part of an espionage scheme. But they didn't have much else to go on, even after a long investigation. But one thing was for sure—New Yorkers had a spy in their midst.

About a year later, a Soviet secret agent, Reino Hayhanen, turned himself in to U.S. agents. He began telling the FBI about

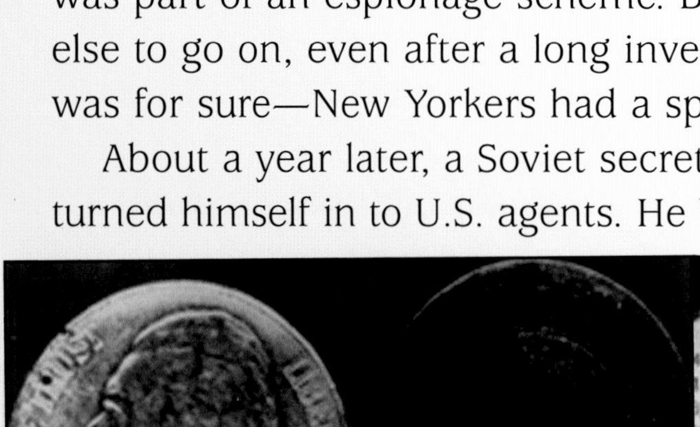

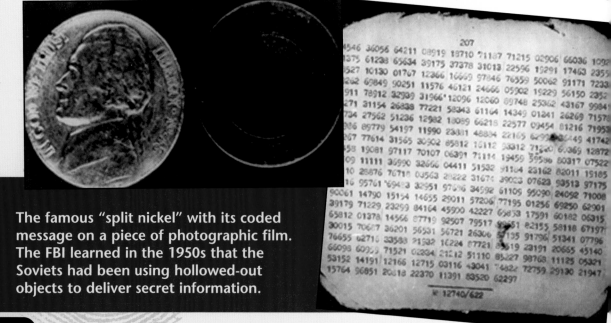

The famous "split nickel" with its coded message on a piece of photographic film. The FBI learned in the 1950s that the Soviets had been using hollowed-out objects to deliver secret information.

a way that Soviet spies carried secret information. The spies would hollow out ordinary objects, like pens, screws, and batteries. Then they put important information or a message inside the objects. The method had proven useful to the spies.

The nickel the newsboy had turned over to authorities fit into that scheme, and Hayhanen knew a man who used those types of objects to spy on the United States. He said he could lead the FBI to the man. The FBI didn't find the man right away. After much detective work, however, the FBI found him in 1957. The man went by the name of William Fisher, but he was also known as Rudolf Abel. He had been involved in Soviet spy operations in the United States since the 1940s. Fisher sometimes ran spy missions himself, but he also recruited and trained other spies for the USSR.

Fisher wouldn't talk to the FBI, but special agents found all sorts of espionage equipment and documents in his home and office. Fisher was convicted of espionage charges in a U.S. court in 1957. He was sentenced to 30 years in prison. In 1962, the United States sent Fisher back to the USSR in a prisoner exchange for U.S. pilot Francis Gary Powers. Powers had been shot down flying over the USSR in a U-2 spy plane in 1960 and was being held captive by the Soviets.

The Vietnam Era

Throughout the 1960s, the Cold War raged. The FBI had to concentrate on counterintelligence. But agents were also directed to watch the actions of domestic groups that in the eyes of the government posed threats to national security.

The FBI was keeping a close eye on Soviet spy operations. The Soviets were seeking top-secret information on U.S. involvement in the Vietnam War. During that war, the United States was trying to stop the spread of communism in North Vietnam to South Vietnam. The USSR supported North Vietnam, and the United States had become the major ally of South Vietnam.

By the late 1960s, many people in the United States had begun to speak out against the Vietnam War. This prompted large antiwar demonstrations all across the United States. Most of these demonstrations were peaceful. But some became violent. It was the FBI's job to watch any groups that used violence to get their message across.

J. Edgar Hoover once said, "In the United States, the **subversive** is a lawbreaker when he violates the law of the land, not because he disagrees with the party in power." As protests against the war continued, however, the FBI also became involved in monitoring the activities of antiwar activists whose words were strong even if their methods were nonviolent.

Radical groups had managed to plant and explode bombs in government buildings like the U.S. Capitol and the Pentagon (the home of the U.S. Department of Defense) in the late 1960s and early 1970s. In 1970 alone, there were an estimated 3,000 bombings in the United States, with another 50,000 bomb threats. The FBI was called in on many of these cases, and the agents treated them as cases of domestic terrorism.

No Limits

During this troubled period, neither the U.S. Congress nor the Justice Department set any guidelines for the FBI to follow in conducting national security probes. The FBI used its **covert** operation called COINTELPRO (Counterintelligence Program)

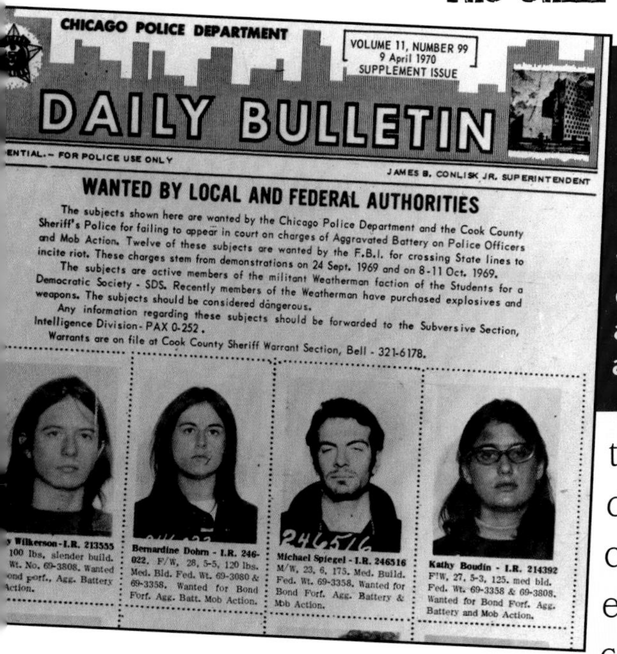

CHICAGO POLICE DEPARTMENT

VOLUME 11, NUMBER 99
9 April 1970
SUPPLEMENT ISSUE

DAILY BULLETIN

ENTIAL.– FOR POLICE USE ONLY

JAMES B. CONLISK JR. SUPERINTENDENT

WANTED BY LOCAL AND FEDERAL AUTHORITIES

The subjects shown here are wanted by the Chicago Police Department and the Cook County Sheriff's Police for failing to appear in court on charges of Aggravated Battery on Police Officers and Mob Action. Twelve of these subjects are wanted by the F.B.I. for crossing State lines to incite riot. These charges stem from demonstrations on 24 Sept. 1969 and on 8-11 Oct. 1969.

The subjects are active members of the militant Weatherman faction of the Students for a Democratic Society - SDS. Recently members of the Weatherman have purchased explosives and weapons. The subjects should be considered dangerous.

Any information regarding these subjects should be forwarded to the Subversive Section, Intelligence Division- PAX 0-252.

Warrants are on file at Cook County Sheriff Warrant Section, Bell - 321-6178.

y Wilkerson-I.R. 213555 100 lbs. slender build. Wt. No. 69-3808. Wanted ond porf., Agg. Battery Action.

Bernardine Dohrn - I.R. 246-022. F/W, 28, 5-5, 120 lbs. Med. Bld. Fed. Wt. 69-3080 & 69-3358. Wanted for Bond Forf. Agg. Batt. Mob Action.

Michael Spiegel - I.R. 246516 M/W, 23, 6, 175. Med. Build. Fed. Wt. 69-3358. Wanted for Bond Forf. Agg. Battery & Mob Action.

Kathy Boudin - I.R. 214392 F/W, 27, 5-3, 125. med bld. Fed. Wt. 69-3358 & 69-3808. Wanted for Bond Forf. Agg. Battery and Mob Action.

One purpose of COINTELPRO was to disrupt the activities of groups the government considered subversive or violent. The people pictured on this bulletin issued by the Chicago Police Department in 1970 were members of the Weathermen, a radical group that sometimes used explosives and other weapons as part of its campaign against the Vietnam War.

to infiltrate, disrupt, and create dissension within various radical groups. COINTELPRO was established in 1956 with the consent of the National Security Council. It was primarily designed to disrupt the activities of communist groups operating within the United States. To a much smaller degree, it was also used to infiltrate and investigate white hate organizations, such as the Ku Klux Klan and various Nazi groups.

In 1967, the program was used to infiltrate a black nationalist group called the Black Panther Party, and it was also used against many groups associated with the civil rights movement and with other less radical causes that the agency deemed as dangerous to society or capable of committing acts of domestic terrorism. Some of these organizations, including those associated with civil rights leader Martin Luther King, Jr., were neither violent nor associated with radical groups on either the right or the left. They were simply longtime objects of Bureau chief J. Edgar Hoover's suspicions and distrust.

COINTELPRO remained a secret operation until 1971, when a group of radicals broke into an FBI field office in

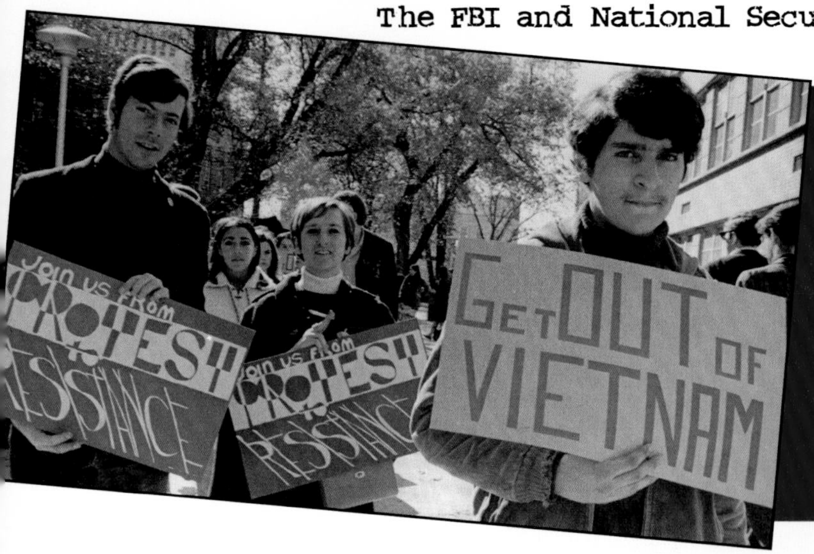

During the late 1960s, the actions of antiwar activists, along with those of people in the civil rights movement, often became the target of COINTELPRO. Most of these activists were not violent, but they attracted the Bureau's attention because of their opposition to government policies.

Media, Pennsylvania, and stole files relating to the operation. They turned the files over to reporters and Congress. Many news outlets published the files, and soon they attracted the unwanted attention of members of Congress as well.

Investigating the Investigators

Hoover ended COINTELPRO shortly after the 1971 break-in. Congress investigated COINTELPRO after the Hoover's death in 1972 and released its findings in 1976. Its report criticized the FBI for overstepping its bounds in going after suspected subversives and domestic terrorists. The report said that the Bureau had violated citizens' First Amendment rights when it came to freedom of speech and freedom of association.

Clarence Kelley became director of the FBI in July 1973. He wanted the Bureau to focus more on doing solid investigative work. He felt this was better than just running up the numbers of cases being investigated. In 1976, Kelley worked with Congress and Attorney General Edward Levi to set up guidelines for FBI investigations. They were especially interested in guidelines for cases dealing with domestic and international intelligence gathering. Kelley hoped that this would fix the problems that Congress had seen with operations like COINTELPRO. He also hoped his actions would restore confidence in the FBI.

Foreign Intelligence Surveillance Act

In 1978, the U.S. Congress passed the Foreign Intelligence Surveillance Act. This law set up the rules for physical and electronic intelligence gathering. It also provided for judicial and congressional oversight of the country's covert intelligence-gathering operations. The law set limits but tried to leave room for the agents to do their jobs.

In 1983, former Judge William Webster was serving as director of the FBI. He worked with Attorney General William French Smith to revise the Levi Guidelines. His goal was to enhance the Bureau's ability to conduct intelligence investigations. The next year, Congress allowed the FBI to chase spies and terrorists beyond U.S. shores if the Bureau believed that they were bent on attacking the United States.

During the 1980s, agents unearthed and arrested the greatest number of spies since World War II. In 1984, a total of 12 people were charged as spies. More were arrested and prosecuted in 1985—so many that the news media dubbed 1985 the Year of the Spy.

Tracking a Hijacker

In June 1985, Lebanese terrorist Fawaz Younis led a team of hijackers who took over a Jordanian airliner in June 1985. The plane had 70 passengers on board, including several Americans. The hijackers seized the plane as it was waiting to take off from the Beirut International Airport in Lebanon. The passengers were eventually released, but the terrorists blew

TERRORISM IN THE SKY

The flight started out as a normal holiday flight on December 21, 1988, but it turned into one of the worst acts of international terrorism ever when Pan Am Flight 103 exploded in midair over Lockerbie, Scotland.

The flight took off from Heathrow Airport in London and was headed to New York City. The plane had 259 passengers and crew aboard. Less than 40 minutes into the flight, the plane exploded, killing all 259 passengers and crewmembers on board plus 11 Scots on the ground. Among the dead were 189 Americans. Debris fell over 845 square miles (2,200 sq km), making the investigation one of the most complex in the history of the FBI.

Police agencies from many countries took part in the investigation. Among these was Britain's famous Scotland Yard. Agents worked on their hands and knees to locate evidence from the bombing. They interviewed more than 10,000 people in connection with the case. The painstaking work paid off. Agents found a fragment (shown below) from the circuit board of a radio/cassette player on the ground. They determined that a bomb had been placed inside the radio. (See photo of a model of the radio below.) The radio was then hidden in a piece of luggage.

The evidence led to two men from Libya. The men were charged by both the United States and Scotland in 1991. Years of discussion with the Libyan government followed. Finally, in 1999, the two men were turned over to Scottish police at a neutral site in the Netherlands. A trial began in May 2000 under Scottish jurisdiction. On January 31, 2001, Abdel Basset Ali Al-Megrahi (shown in the mug shot below) was found guilty of the crimes that resulted in the blowing up of Flight 103. The second suspect was found not guilty.

The Libyan government eventually admitted responsibility for the crime and paid $3 billion to the victims' families.

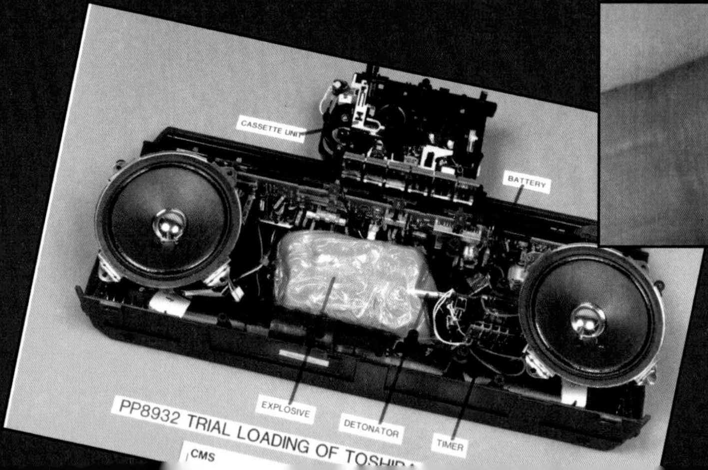

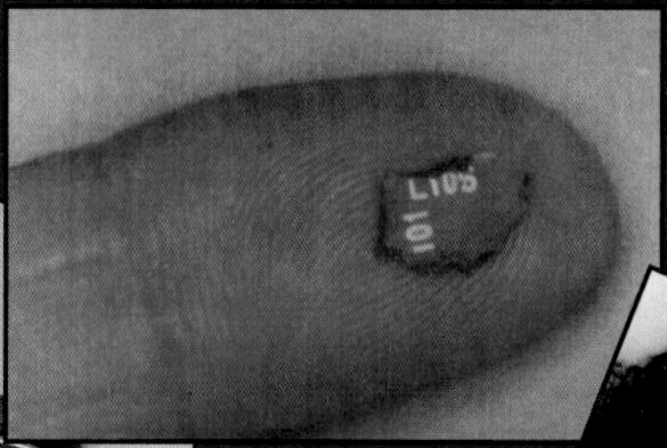

up the plane and fled. Younis served as the spokesperson for the group and appeared on TV.

In September 1987, using the congressional authority they had been given to go overseas in pursuit of terrorists who had plans to attack the United States, FBI special agents set a trap. Lured to a yacht in international waters in the Mediterranean Sea off Cyprus, Younis thought he was meeting with an international drug dealer. The "dealer" had promised to help him raise money for more terrorist activity through a **lucrative** illegal drug operation. All of the people on the yacht were FBI agents. After Younis spent some time there, the agents moved in. They arrested him and took him back to the United States for trial.

In October 1989, Younis was convicted of aircraft piracy, conspiracy, and hostage taking. He was sentenced to 30 years in prison.

The End of the Cold War, a New Era in Security Concerns

In 1989, communist nations in Eastern Europe had begun moving away from their allegiance to the Soviet Union and were on their way toward becoming democracies more similar to those in Western Europe. With the lessening influence of the USSR in Europe, tensions between the United States and Soviet Union also began to ease. In 1991, the Soviet Union dissolved, effectively bringing a complete end to the Cold War. Though the FBI was no longer battling Soviet spies, there was still counterintelligence work to be done. Soon the faces of international terrorists would replace the faces of Soviet spies on FBI Most Wanted posters. National security interests were about to become more critical—and complex—than ever.

CHAPTER 5 A Very Dangerous World

When a car bomb went off in the parking garage below the North Tower (Tower One) of the World Trade Center in New York City on February 26, 1993, no one had imagined that an office complex, even one with two buildings more than 100 stories high, was in the process of becoming a very special target for terrorists. No one knew until some time later that even then terrorists were trying to topple the giant structure. The blast caused death, damage, fear, and confusion, but the terrorists wanted much more. They wanted to make a statement against the United States of America.

Investigators dig through the rubble of the bombing of the World Trade Center in 1993. The blast occurred when explosives placed beneath the Twin Towers were detonated. It created a hole six stories deep.

The FBI was on the scene in moments. The New York City Police Department was, too. More than 700 FBI special agents worldwide eventually worked the case. Investigators at the scene quickly recovered a key piece of evidence that led to an arrest several days after the blast.

A Big Break

In the rubble was a vehicle identification number. Investigators traced the number to a rented truck that had been used in the bombing. On March 4, only days after the blast, a team of FBI agents arrested Mohammad Salameh, an Islamic fundamentalist. They captured him at the truck rental store in Jersey City, New Jersey, where he had rented the vehicle. Salameh was trying—unsuccessfully—to get back the $400 deposit he had put down on the truck. His arrest was a big break in the case.

The FBI special agents learned that the mastermind behind the attack was a man born in Kuwait of Pakistani descent named Ramzi Yousef. Yousef freely admitted that he had intended for the North Tower to collapse onto its twin, the South Tower. The blast was timed to take place in the middle of the workday. If all had gone according to his plan, he figured that 250,000 people or more could have been killed. In addition, Yousef claimed to have put deadly cyanide gas in the bomb planted in the rented truck. The cyanide was supposed to have been released when the bomb went off. He planned for it to circulate throughout Lower Manhattan after the buildings had come crashing down. More people would have been killed as dusty air from the explosion swirled around the city.

Fortunately, the plot didn't work as planned. The blast was bad enough. It killed six people and injured 1,042 more. It also created a crater six stories deep in the basement below the North Tower. The blast knocked out power to the World Trade Center and sent thick, heavy smoke up to the 93rd floor, including into the stairwells. Hundreds of people were stuck in elevators. Evacuating the scene was difficult, but, miraculously, it was done with relatively few casualties.

Yousef and all but one of his co-conspirators (shown at left) were caught. Yousef was arrested in Pakistan in February 1995 and returned to the United States. At the time of his arrest, he was planning a series of attacks on U.S. airliners. The terrorists were tried in court, convicted, and given long sentences for their crime.

Terror in Oklahoma City

Just two years later, on April 19, 1995, the FBI was called in to investigate the worst case of domestic terrorism to date. A normal workday in Oklahoma City

The force of the explosion in front of the federal building in Oklahoma City ripped off the entire face of the building from top to bottom. It also destroyed most of the vehicles parked nearby.

turned into a nightmare when the Alfred P. Murrah Federal Building was blown up. The weapon was a rented truck, loaded with powerful explosives. It had been parked outside the building and was detonated just after 9:00 A.M. More than 800 people were injured. Another 168 were killed, including children in the first-floor day-care center. At first many thought the bombing was an act of foreign terrorism.

Once again, the FBI found a vehicle identification number in the rubble. The agents traced it to a Junction City, Kansas, body shop. At the shop, employees helped the FBI put together a **composite** drawing (near right) of the man who had rented the truck used in the bombing. Then the agents showed the drawing around Junction City. Hotel employees gave them a name—26-year-old Timothy McVeigh (far right).

Agents started their search for McVeigh at once. They were startled to find out that he was already in jail. Just after the bombing, McVeigh had been pulled over by an Oklahoma state trooper; his vehicle had no license plate. The trooper found that McVeigh was carrying a concealed gun and arrested him for that. The FBI soon charged McVeigh with the bombing. They also arrested a friend of his, Terry Nichols, and charged him with helping build the bomb. The FBI learned that both men were extremists who hated the U.S. government.

In 1997, McVeigh was found guilty of the bombing. He was sentenced to death for the crime and was executed by lethal injection in June 2001. Nichols stood trial separately.

He was also found guilty and sentenced to life in prison without the possibility of parole. As it turned out, the Oklahoma City bombing was not an act of international terrorism. It did serve, however, as a terrifying reminder that national security can be threatened both from inside and outside the United States.

FAST FACTS

On September 12, 2005, the FBI established a National Security Branch made up of the Counterterrorism Division, the Counterintelligence Division, the Directorate of Intelligence, the Terrorist Screening Center, and the Weapons of Mass Destruction Directorate.

African Embassy Bombings

Terrorists bombed U.S. embassies in Dar es Salaam, Tanzania, and Nairobi, Kenya, on August 7, 1998. Nearly 1,000 FBI special agents were called in to investigate. The nearly simultaneous bombings injured more than 4,500 people and killed 224, including 12 Americans. Four terrorists linked to al-Qaeda (the group tied to the attacks of September 11, 2001) were arrested for their roles in the bombings and tried in a U.S. court. They were found guilty in 2000 and given life sentences. Other suspects are still being sought.

The FBI was upgrading its approach to counterterrorism and intelligence gathering even before the 9/11 attacks occurred. The attacks increased the need. FBI Director Robert S. Mueller III summed up the agency's new mission by saying,

The blast that heavily damaged the U.S. embassy in Nairobi, Kenya, also destroyed these vehicles parked nearby. The perfectly timed nature of the explosions in Kenya and Tanzania would become a trademark of al-Qaeda, the group responsible for the attacks of 9/11.

> Working closely with our partners in intelligence, law enforcement, military and diplomatic circles, the FBI's primary responsibility is to neutralize terrorist cells and operatives here in the United States and help dismantle terrorist networks worldwide.

Key Lesson: Prevention

The key lesson of 9/11 was the need for prevention. That lesson has helped the FBI change to meet the national security challenges of the 21st century. The Bureau has sharpened its ability to predict and prevent acts of terrorism. This is due, in part, to better communication with law enforcement partners. But it also has to do with modernizing technology, expanding intelligence capabilities, and revamping the counterterrorism operation.

Since the attacks of 9/11, the FBI has more than doubled the number of special agents working on terrorism to a present total of over 2,500 people. But every special agent in the Bureau also has the skills to handle a terrorism case. The Bureau has also increased the number of intelligence analysts working on counterterrorism by transferring some of its own analysts from other divisions into counterterrorism and mixing analysts from other government agencies, such as the CIA, into its counterterrorism operation.

Counterterrorism analysts for the Bureau can analyze data from one investigation and see how it might cast light on another. The FBI also has added hundreds more foreign language translators since 9/11. More than 75 percent of those translators are experts in Middle Eastern languages. Most of the Middle Eastern translators are native speakers in those languages. This means they are familiar with slang and **colloquial** speech, so nothing is lost in translation.

In addition, native speakers working as translators are familiar with cultural, historical, and religious references. This gives their translations a deeper, more substantive meaning. The translators are backed up by over 1,000 special agents who have a minimal working knowledge of these foreign languages as well.

Counterterrorism Watch Unit

The FBI has established a Counterterrorism Watch Unit (CT Watch). This unit gathers information from different sources about threats to national security. Some threats come from within the nation's borders, and some come from overseas. Information comes in from foreign sources as well as national, state, and even municipal law enforcement officials. All information gathered by CT Watch is evaluated for urgency and credibility. It is then assigned to an FBI division for further investigation. CT Watch follows up with the various divisions that are handling the leads. This way, the unit maintains the latest information on those investigations.

Another focus of the Bureau's counterterrorism operation is the Correctional Intelligence Initiative. This program is coordinated through the National Joint Terrorism Task Force (NJTTF). It recruits prison inmates who may have had contacts or sources within domestic radical groups or within anti-American groups in foreign countries. Inmates are asked to share any information they might have about ongoing activities by enemies of the United States. Some inmates have insight into a group's ability to harm the country. The program has turned up a number of valuable leads.

Operation TRIPWIRE is yet another prevention initiative. It targets terrorist sleeper cells. The operation collects information on the training, financing, and recruitment of terrorists. It also works to uncover any plots these terrorists might be planning. For example, Operation TRIPWIRE has focused on agricultural aviation. The Federal Aviation Administration gave the FBI a list of more than 11,000 registered aircraft used for agricultural purposes, most of them crop dusters. The FBI had information that some of these crop dusters might be used by terrorists. These airplanes could be used to spread poisons over a wide area. FBI agents interviewed many of the crop duster owners and operators. Several investigations were

Crop dusting planes are a real threat as a delivery system for bioterrorism. Since the attacks of 9/11, the FBI has established contacts with the agricultural aviation industry to keep tabs on possible sleeper agents having access to planes such as the one shown here.

OFFENSE IS THE BEST DEFENSE

Here is just one of the ways that post-9/11 intelligence gathering is designed to make the United States safer from the threat of terrorist activity.

Ziad Jarrah was speeding near the Maryland state line on September 9, 2001. He was pulled over by a Maryland state trooper. It was a rather routine traffic stop. The state trooper checked Jarrah's license and registration against the database for outstanding warrants. The check came back clean, and soon Jarrah was back on his way. He was in a hurry to join the rest of the September 11 terrorists who were going to hijack United Flight 93, the plane that crashed in a field in Pennsylvania. The Maryland state trooper had no idea that Jarrah was on the CIA's watch list.

Today, that database check would have gone much differently. If a law enforcement officer anywhere in the country stopped Jarrah, his identification information would raise a red flag in the FBI's National Crime Information Center (NCIC). He would automatically be checked against a database of suspected terrorists. Because Jarrah's name was on the list, the trooper would be instructed to get in touch with the FBI's Terrorist Screening Center (TSC) immediately. He would continue to detain but not arrest the suspect.

In moments, TSC officials would determine whether Jarrah was the person the intelligence community was seeking. If so, the unit would ask the trooper to briefly question the suspect at the traffic stop. Then members of the area's Joint Terrorism Task Force would most likely be sent to the scene.

The Ziad Jarrah story highlighted one weakness in the FBI's counterterrorism operation. Sadly, that weakness was discovered after 9/11. The basic problem was that the various government and law enforcement agencies dealing with counterterrorism had no way to share information about suspected terrorists. As a result, in the pre-9/11 world, Jarrah fell through the cracks. In the post-9/11 world, he would not.

Since the attacks of 9/11, a police officer making a routine traffic stop would have quick access to the FBI's National Crime Information Center (NCIC) and Terrorist Screening Center (TSC), shown at left. Within moments, that officer would be given any information—and assistance—needed to identify and detain anyone whose record raises concerns about possible terrorist connections.

opened as a result of this work. The agricultural aviation aircraft list is constantly reviewed.

FAST FACTS

Among its other programs to combat terrorism, the FBI's Maritime Threat Project is planned to prevent and disrupt attacks on the high seas. Another program—the Bioterrorism Risk Assessment Group—is meant to thwart terrorist attacks using biological agents or toxins.

Up-to-Date Technical Support

The FBI's Investigative Technology Division (ITD), established in August 2002, grew out of the Bureau's Laboratory Division. The ITD provides the most up-to-date technical information to back up the FBI's investigations. The division is also expected to develop new investigative technologies. ITD plays an important role in the collection and processing of intelligence information gathered from computers as well as audio and video equipment.

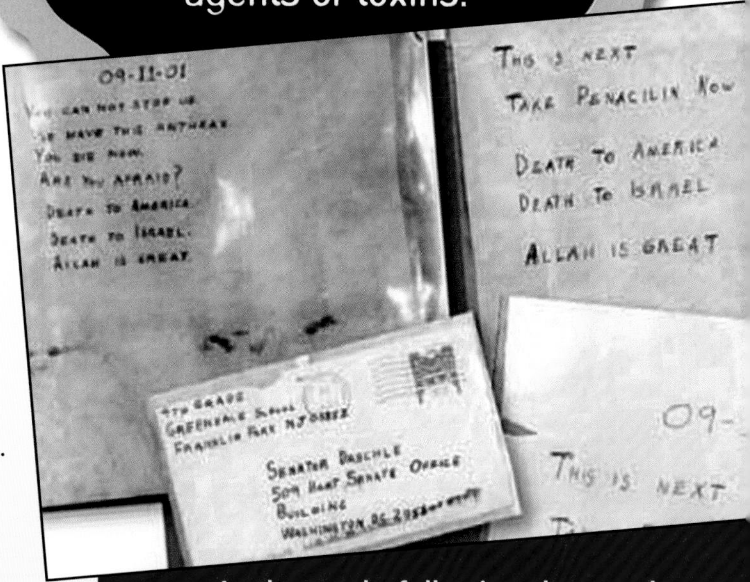

In the weeks following the attacks of 9/11, the United States was subjected to what the FBI describes as "the most significant bioterrorist attack in the nation's history." This attack, a form of bioterrorism, consisted of anthrax-tainted letters mailed to members of Congress and the media. By the end of 2001, 18 cases of anthrax were confirmed. Of those cases, five resulted in deaths.

The FBI has developed strong partnerships with counter-terrorism and law enforcement agencies both in the United States and abroad. FBI special agents constantly share vital information with state and local law enforcement agencies in the United States, and with other federal agencies. Among these are the Department of Homeland Security, the CIA, and all branches of the military.

The FBI established the National Media Exploitation Center in 2001. Millions of documents, videotapes, and audiotapes have been seized by the U.S. military and counterintelligence agencies in foreign lands, especially Afghanistan. These items must be analyzed for leads and intelligence information. They also must be checked for fingerprints and DNA. The center coordinates that effort and distributes the information drawn from those documents.

"Strategic" Response

These are just some of the post-9/11 changes that the FBI has put in place to safeguard national security. As Director Mueller has said,

> Our response to terrorism is now strategic, with our annual international terrorism threat assessments providing strategic warning of the most critical threats, identifying key gaps in intelligence, and pinpointing emerging operational trends that require immediate collection and analysis.

In short, the FBI must be on the alert on more fronts than ever before, and on a 24/7 basis.

CHRONOLOGY

1901: President William McKinley is shot in Buffalo, New York, and dies eight days later.

1914: World War I begins.

1916: German saboteurs bomb the Black Tom railroad yard, a depot for munitions made in the northeast United States, in New Jersey.

1917: The Bureau discovers that Germany has hidden important documents containing information about Germany's war activities in the Swiss Consulate in New York City.

The United States declares war on the Central Powers and enters World War I.

1918: World War I ends.

1920: New York's Lower Manhattan is bombed when a horse-drawn wagon explodes on Wall St. across from the J.P. Morgan Bank.

1941: Fritz Duquesne and 32 members of his German spy ring are arrested.

Japanese planes bomb the U.S. Pacific Fleet in Pearl Harbor, Hawaii, on December 7, drawing the United States into World War II.

1945: World War II ends.

1945–1991: The Cold War.

1956: The FBI Counterintelligence Program, known as COINTELPRO, is established.

1980: The FBI's first Joint Terrorism Task Force (JTTF) is established in New York City.

1985: Fawaz Younis leads a team of hijackers in the takeover of a Jordanian airliner.

1987: FBI sets a trap for Lebanese terrorist Fawaz Younis. Agents use the congressional authority they had been given to go after terrorists overseas who had designs on attacking the United States. Younis will be convicted of aircraft piracy, conspiracy, and hostage taking and sentenced to 30 years in prison.

1991: The Soviet Union dissolves, effectively ending the Cold War.

1993: New York City's World Trade Center is attacked in a car bombing in the parking garage below the North Tower.

1995: The Alfred P. Murrah Federal Building in Oklahoma City is blown up in the worst case of domestic terrorism ever. More than 800 people are injured; 168 are killed.

1997: Timothy McVeigh is found guilty of the Oklahoma City bombing and is sentenced to death. His associate Terry Nichols is found guilty on charges of conspiracy and sentenced to life in prison without parole.

1998: Terrorists bomb U.S. embassies in Tanzania and Kenya.

2001: September 11: Terrorists hijack four U.S. jetliners. All four crash, three into buildings and one into a field, killing all passengers and crew plus people in the buildings.

2009: In April, animal-rights extremist Daniel Andreas San Diego becomes the first domestic terrorist named to the FBI's Most Wanted Terrorists list. He is wanted on charges related to bombing two buildings.

GLOSSARY

anthrax—a bacterial disease that usually affects livestock but can be transmitted to humans, causing severe skin and lung problems. The use of anthrax as a terrorist weapon has been a cause for concern following the attacks of 9/11.

asylum—a place of refuge and protection; refugees often seek asylum in a country such as the United States.

bastion—stronghold; mainstay.

billow—to swell; rise, as in waves.

colloquial—informal, as in spoken or written words.

communists—people who believe in a system in which the government owns all property and makes all economic decisions; can also refer to a political party based on these beliefs.

composite—a blend of several elements or parts.

counterintelligence—intelligence agency activity that counters, or blocks, its enemy's intelligence activity. This may include an enemy's attempts to gather information, engage in harmful acts, or otherwise do damage.

covert—secret; done out of public view.

fascist—having to do with a political organization that is brutally dictatorial and authoritarian and is intolerant of any opposition to its policies. Fascist governments also tend to uphold the supremacy of one national or ethnic group over all others.

foil—to stop; to break up, as a plot.

freeze the assets—to prevent individuals, businesses, or governments from gaining access to funds in their own bank accounts.

imminent—happening immediately or very soon.

intelligence—information of political or military value; the collection of that information.

internment—imprisonment in camps.

lucrative—highly profitable.

munitions—ammunition, especially larger varieties such as rockets or bombs.

psyche—a collective way of thinking.

restitution—reimbursement or repayment for a loss or injury.

sabotage—deliberate acts of destruction, damage, or obstruction, usually for military reasons.

saboteurs—people involved in sabotage.

shrapnel—small pieces of metal released from a bomb or as part of an explosion.

Soviet Union—officially the Union of Soviet Socialist Republics (USSR); a communist nation created in Eastern Europe and Central Asia following the revolution in Russia in 1917 that became a major superpower following the end of World War II in 1945. In 1991, the Soviet Union broke up into numerous independent republics, including Russia, Ukraine, Kazakhstan, Armenia, and Georgia.

subversive—someone working secretly, sometimes within the political system, to overthrow the government.

treasonous—having to do with the crime of betraying one's country.

turf war—dispute over who is in charge, usually between two people or organizations.

unconstitutional—in violation of the constitution or some other set of laws.

vigilant—watchful; alert to danger.

FURTHER READING

Batvinis, Raymond J. *The Origins of FBI Counterintelligence*. Lawrence: University Press of Kansas, 2007.

Coulson, Daniel, and Sharon Shannon. *No Heroes: Inside the FBI's Secret Counter-Terror Force*. New York: Pocket Books, 2001.

Holden, Henry M. *FBI 100 Years: An Unofficial History*. Minneapolis: Zenith Press, 2008.

Jeffreys-Jones, Rhodri. *The FBI: A History*. New Haven, CT: Yale University Press, 2008.

National Commission on Terrorist Attacks. *The 9/11 Commission Report: Final Report of the National Commission on Terrorist Attacks upon the United States*. New York: W. W. Norton & Co., 2004.

Volkman, Ernest. *Espionage: The Greatest Spy Operations of the Twentieth Century*. New York: John Wiley & Sons, 1996.

Witover, Jules. *Sabotage at Black Tom: Imperial Germany's Secret War in America 1914–1917*. Chapel Hill, NC: Algonquin Books, 1989.

INTERNET RESOURCES

http://www.fbi.gov

This is the official site of the FBI. It contains the history of the Bureau's work in the area of national security. It also has press releases about the agency's latest efforts to protect the nation and recent investigations into national security breaches.

http://www.usdoj.gov

This is the official site of the U.S. Department of Justice. It includes press releases and the latest information about action being taken to protect the nation from terrorist attacks.

http://www.nsa.gov

This is the Web site of the National Security Agency. It provides information on what the agency does to protect national security.

http://www.cia.gov

The Web site of the Central Intelligence Agency has historical information about intelligence gathering and how it has changed over time. The site also contains information on the agency today.

http://www.whitehouse.gov/nsc/

The National Security Council advises the president on issues of national security. This site contains information about the work of the council throughout its history.

http://www.dhs.gov

The Department of Homeland Security handles issues of national security. This site contains press releases about the work of the department in all areas of homeland security, from internal threats to natural disasters.

NOTES

Chapter 1

p. 8: "The failure to prevent . . .": Thomas L. Friedman, "A Failure to Imagine," *New York Times* (May 19, 2002), http://query.nytimes.com/gst/fullpage.html?res=950CEFDE1738F93AA25756C0A9649C8B63.

p. 11: "The enemies we face . . .": Robert S. Mueller III, Director, FBI, Testimony Before the Select Committee on Intelligence of the United States Senate, February 11, 2003, http://www.fbi.gov/congress/congress03/mueller021103.htm.

Chapter 2

p. 18 "[t]he United States must be neutral in . . .": Woodrow Wilson, President Wilson's Declaration of Neutrality Before the 63rd Congress, August 19, 1914, http://wwi.lib.byu.edu/index.php/President_Wilson%27s_Declaration_of_Neutrality.

p. 20: "I never believed such a thing . . .": "How Witnesses Survived Explosion," *New York Times* (July 31, 1916), http://query.nytimes.com/gst/abstract.html?res=9A04E1DC1E3FE233A25752C3A9619C946796D6CF.

Chapter 3

p. 26: "The lessons to America are as clear . . .": Quoted by Michael Daly, "A Lesson in History and Baseball," *New York Daily News* (October 12, 2003), http://www.nydailynews.com/archives/news/2003/10/12/2003-10-12_a_lesson_in_history_and_base.html.

p. 26: "tear out the radical seeds . . .": A. Mitchell Palmer, "The Case Against the 'Reds,'" *Forum* 63 (1920): 173–185.

Chapter 4

p. 40: "In the United States, the subversive . . .": Ray Wannall, *The Real J. Edgar Hoover for the Record* (Paducah, KY: Turner Publications, 2000), p. 32.

Chapter 5

p. 51: "Working closely with our partners in intelligence . . .": Robert S. Mueller III, Director, FBI, Statement Before the Senate Select Committee on Intelligence, January 11, 2007, http://www.fbi.gov/congress/congress07/mueller011107.htm.

p. 56: "Our response to terrorism . . .": Robert S. Mueller III, Director, FBI, Press Release, "The Terrorist Threat and Our Concerted Response," September 10, 2007, http://www.fbi.gov/page2/sept07/threat091007.htm.

INDEX

About the Author

Robert Grayson is an award-winning former daily newspaper reporter and the author of a book of crime victims' services called *The Crime Victim's Aid*. Among the hundreds of articles he has written are pieces on the judicial system, including "Criminal Justice Vs. Victim Justice: A Need to Balance the Scales," published in the *Justice Reporter*. Throughout his journalism career, Robert has written stories on sports, arts and entertainment, business, pets, and profiles. His work has appeared in national and regional publications.